Exploring Earth's Resources

Using Air

Sharon Katz Cooper

Heinemann Library
Chicago, Illinois

Customer Service   888–363–4266

Visit our website at www.heinemannraintree.com

Designed by Michelle Lisseter
Printed and bound in China, by South China Printing Company

11 10 09 08 07
10 9 8 7 6 5 4 3 2 1

Library of Congress Cataloging-in-Publication Data

Katz Cooper, Sharon.
  Using air / Sharon Katz Cooper.
     p. cm. -- (Exploring Earth's resources)
  Includes index.
  ISBN-13: 978-1-4034-9315-6 (lib. bdg.)
  ISBN-10: 1-4034-9315-4 (lib. bdg.)
  ISBN-13: 978-1-4034-9323-1 (pbk.)
  ISBN-10: 1-4034-9323-5 (pbk.)
 1. Air--Juvenile literature. I. Title.
  QC161.2.K38 2007
  551.5--dc22

                                    2006029661

Acknowledgments
The publishers would like to thank the following for permission to reproduce photographs:
Alamy p. 12 (Travel Ink); Corbis pp. 4 (NASA), 5 (Zefa/Alexander Benz), 7, 9 (Warren Faidley), 14 (Walter Geiersperger), 20 (Issei Kato); Getty Images pp. 6 (Iconica), 8 (Photographer's Choice/Brian Stablyk), 10 (Stone), 13 (Photodisc), 15 (Nancy Sefton), 18 (Stone/Jeremy Walker); Harcourt Education Ltd p. 22 (Tudor Photography); Photoedit p. 11 (Tony Freeman); Photolibrary p. 21 (Goodshot); Science Photo Library pp. 16 (British Antarctic Survey), 17 (David Hay Jones); Still Photos p. 19 (Mark Edwards).

Cover photograph reproduced with permission of Getty Images (Stockbyte Silver).

Every effort has been made to contact copyright holders of any material reproduced in this book. Any omissions will be rectified in subsequent printings if notice is given to the publishers.

Contents

Some words are shown in bold, **like this**.
You can find them in the glossary on page 23.

What Is Air?

Air is all around us. Air is a layer
of gases around Earth.

air bubbles

Air is a **natural resource**.

Natural resources come from Earth.

How Do We Know Air Is All Around Us?

We cannot see air, but we can feel it and use it.

We can watch it move a kite.

Wind is air that is moving.

We can see the wind blow trees.

What Is Air Made Of?

Air is not nothing. It is a mixture of gases.

Helium is one of the gases in air. We often use it to fill balloons.

Oxygen is an important gas in air. We need it to breathe.

Water **vapor** is another gas in air. Fog is made of water vapor you can see.

How Do We Use Air?

Humans and animals breathe air.

Our bodies need **oxygen** to stay alive.

Air goes into our lungs when we breathe in.

We can blow it out into a balloon.

Plants need air, too.

They use carbon dioxide gas from air to make food.

Plants also put **oxygen** back into air.

Humans and animals need oxygen to breathe.

People use air to make **energy**.
Wind makes windmills turn.

The windmills produce electricity.

We also use air to have fun.

Scuba divers use tanks of air to dive deep in the ocean.

Who Studies Air?

Scientists who study air are called meteorologists.

They look at wind and how air moves.

Other scientists study gases and dirt in the air.

They find ways to keep air cleaner.

Can We Run Out of Air?

We cannot run out of air, but air can get dirty.

Using **fossil fuels** causes air **pollution**.

Dirty air can make people sick. It can cause **asthma** and coughing.

How Can We Keep Air Clean?

We can help clean our air by burning fewer **fossil fuels**.

We can drive cleaner cars that use less fuel.

We can sometimes use bikes, buses, and trains instead of cars.

Air Experiment

Now you know that we need air to live. Did you know that fire needs air to burn? We use burning for many things, such as cooking and running engines. Try this experiment to see how fire uses up air.

1. Light a candle in a holder.

2. Place a large glass on top of the candle.

3. Watch to see how long the flame burns.

4. What happened? When the candle has used up the air in the glass, it goes out.

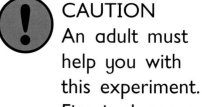

CAUTION
An adult must help you with this experiment. Fire is dangerous. Never play with fire on your own.

Glossary

 **asthma** illness that makes it hard for a person to breathe

 **energy** something that gives power

 **fossil fuel** gas, oil, or coal. Fossil fuels are made from plants and animals that lived long ago.

 **natural resource** material from Earth that we can use

 **oxygen** gas we need to breathe

 **pollution** something that poisons or damages air, water, or land

 **vapor** another word for gas

Index